A Shiny for Trick

S.K. Balk

A Shiny for Trick

Copyright © 2017 S.K. Balk

All rights reserved.

ISBN-13: 9781389855566

A Shiny for Trick

For all of Ms. Gipson's classes.
May you never set limitations on your imagination.

CHAPTER ONE
Of Lost Things and Lost Places

Sometimes we lose things. We've all done it. Car keys, socks, a favorite video, a cherished ring...sometimes we lose them and find them again, in places we didn't expect. Sometimes we lose them and *never* find them again. There is a certain beauty in lost things, like a hope that exists separate from one's self. Somewhere out there, at this time, is a thing you are missing. Perhaps, if you believe in magic, as I do, you believe it misses you, too. You and your one thing are separated, desperately seeking one another.

Maybe the reason you need it is practical. Maybe you need your keys to get to work. Maybe you need your softball glove to play in the game this weekend. Maybe your television doesn't change channels without the remote and you're tired of watching the news. Maybe your life is on hold for that thing you have lost.

Maybe the reason is less practical. Irrational. Emotional. You *need* that thing, though you can't place your finger on exactly why, save that you're *less* without it. Something in *you* is missing until your thing is found. You will live a half-existence, aching for a thing that is lost, one for which you have no idea where to even begin looking. Perhaps you believe that it's lost forever. Perhaps you've cried.

Maybe you still cry.

There's a favored joke going around that when the dryer inexplicably seems to eat socks, they all go someplace special. That perhaps someone, somewhere, is hoarding lost things. A pile of them kept in a secret place just waiting to be discovered. It's a romantic notion, one that promises magic and fae things. But magic both scares and delights us. Believing that there exists such a place upsets the natural order of the universe. Too many things would change if magic was real.

But as it so happens, magic *is* real. In that

state of half-existence you experience when your most-needed thing is gone, magic is *rich*. There are tons of discarded things there. Lost, beautiful things. Things people accidentally dropped or misplaced and could never find again. The moment these things slip from memory, they're lost to the next-to world, a place where things wait to be found again. And this is the realm of special creatures who—unbeknownst to them—exist to bring you your thing back, and it is this strange occupation they crave above all else. Their only instinct is to do this, and in it they find boundless joy.

This is the story about one such creature, and the one such thing that, for a short time, seemed more important to her than anything else.

CHAPTER TWO
Of Boxes and Shiny Things

There is a place, far to the north, where the land believes it is winter for two thirds of every year. The people who live there like to joke about the changes in weather, and will tell you when you go there to pack both a pair of shorts and a sweatshirt. It's a wonderful place. The townsfolk are quick with a smile and eager to help. That's a good quality, when out-of-towners are almost sure to bury themselves in the snow when it hits. Of course, such an event only elicits tired fondness for these bright-eyed tourists. Of course they thought Michigan would be beautiful in the wintertime (it was). Of course they thought they could brave the icy roads (they couldn't) or drive without snow tires (they *really* couldn't). The locals are used to this.

This place is especially wonderful in the summertime, though. Festivals rule the agenda in the summer—festivals about asparagus, fish, cherries, food, movies—and the city swells to many times its original size, near to bursting at the seams for all the people it holds. It is a much cherished time of year, by both the people who live there— most of them, anyway—and the people who would visit.

But it was always a particularly excellent time of year for Trick, for it was a time when more people than she could ever hope to count came to her territory and lost the most wonderful things for her to find. Of course, she didn't know that that was what happened, but she loved it nonetheless.

Trick was a very special creature, with a lovable, huggable nature. She was about two feet tall with dark skin and huge orange faerie eyes. Long, thin, pointed ears stuck out from her head, swiveling with every sound. Upon her head was white hair cut short about her ears by a dulling knife, unkempt. She had no care for her appearance. Everything about herself

A Shiny for Trick

mattered little and less, and no one had ever bothered her with a necessity to know. Her existence was merely that: an existence. It was a quiet, aware one. A private existence. And that suited her just fine.

Trick was what was called a Nomchai, much like wood sprites, except that no one knew they existed. Nomchai were invisible to everyone, even to each other. They had no idea how they came into being and didn't care. Nomchai like Trick only mattered in each moment they existed. Trick was Trick. She didn't even know her real name, though it was probably important. Nonetheless, that was the way of things. She named herself when she heard the word on a breeze one day, clearer than any word ever said. She decided she liked the way it sounded, and that was it. Once the music of it escaped from her lips, she knew with a certainty that she would cherish the word forever, and that's what a name was for. She said the name to herself often, just so she didn't forget. It was the only actual word she ever said.

One might wonder what the purpose of such a creature was. In reality, none will ever know that, either. She probably wasn't, strictly speaking, *necessary*. As the shiny things she loved most probably weren't necessary. Trick didn't care. What Trick did care about was *stuff*. All kinds of stuff. Pretty stuff, shiny stuff, stuff with bows and ribbons, stuff that smelled interesting, stuff she could carry and stuff she couldn't. Every day was a hunt for new stuff, for things that could amuse her for a little while before she found someone who might like that stuff better and gave it away.

Nothing interested Trick more than keys. Lost keys. Every time she found a key she kept it until she found the box it opened. The boxes were always magical and she didn't know how they got there. Trick would find a key and carry it, and eventually she'd find its magical box. The key could be any key: an apartment key, a car key, a key to someone's diary. Any key and every key also had a special magic box, and only Trick could see them. It was entirely possible that other Nomchai could see the boxes, too, but Trick didn't know there *were* other Nomchai. Every key she had was hers, the only one like it. And every key opened exactly one box.

Trick sometimes saw boxes for which she

A Shiny for Trick

had no key. Those days were the hardest. It made her so upset that she would cry for hours. Finding keys was her obsession. Day after day, Trick searched for keys, and the boxes her keys could open. Finding the treasure within brought her the sweetest joy. It didn't matter what kind of treasure lay within. She had no idea what any of it was. But that was just fine. She'd carry it as long as it amused her, and then she'd leave it for someone to find that might enjoy it. She liked the way the people looked when they picked up her treasures.

Today's magical box was flat, broad, and made of shimmering gold. *Shiny, shiny,* she thought, pleased. Shiny boxes often contained shiny, wonderful things. The box glowed faintly as all magical boxes do. It was far out at the end of a stony pier. There were gulls standing next to it, tipping their heads back and making the most wondrous sounds. Trick laughed, a chortling giggle of pure happiness, the pervading emotion at that time. Her toes danced as she capered, delighted to have found such a worthy, beautiful box.

The pier was far out into a lake. On either side of the pier were the misty shadows of opposing shorelines. It made the box feel like even more divine providence. This was a very special box. Trick stood before it, reveling in the moment. The moment she shared with each and every box was intensely special for just that instant. Now was one such. She breathed deeply and grinned. The air from the huge lake smelled fishy, but wonderful. Like damp stone, cold sand, the musty, dusty smell of feathers.

From far off came the fragrance of roasted turkey legs and cherries. Some kind of festival was in full swing. All around her, Trick could see hundreds upon hundreds of people moving to and fro. Trick existed on a different plane, of course. A halfway plane, somewhere between the humans' world and…well, nothing. She could see them moving around like ghosts, photo negatives, muted shadows with garbled voices and blurred out faces. She loved each and every one she saw. Loving the half-real people was part of her joyful existence. Finding them stuff was her game.

She released her deeply held breath, savoring the many flavors upon her tongue. Then her orange eyes popped open, staring at the glory of the giant lake, almost a sea.

A Shiny for Trick

"Trick!" she exclaimed. Then, she knelt before her golden treasure chest and set about opening it up.

Trick carried multitudes of keys with her that jingled constantly as she walked, like the soundtrack of her own personal treasure quest. She kept them hooked together on strings, ribbons, shoelaces and wires. She tied some to her belt, some across her shoulders, still others in her hair. There were keys on her boot laces and keys in her pockets. Keys were the most interesting objects in the world, and she loved them the most. Every key was different. Every key was special. Every key fit in exactly one lock. And together, they made the most glorious music with every step she took.

The only problem with having so many keys was that it took a very long time to find the one for that lock. Upon her forehead was a shoelace that she wore like a crown. It dangled keys in her eyes, so they were the keys that she saw first. She went cross-eyed when she spied them, then grinned with delight and unhooked the lace. She dropped the string too hard on purpose, entertained by the pronounced note of discord as dozens of keys struck stone at once. She giggled, feathering long, delicate fingers over her line of keys askew. They stuck out in all directions like dancers that had fallen over—brass, silver, gold and dingy.

With a deep breath and a hum, she settled on the first key. It was small and square and made a high, sharp note when she struck it against the stone—just because—and she echoed its tone as she spoke her name again. "Trick!" she trilled. Then she held her breath and set key to lock. She pushed. It didn't fit. She frowned and made a disappointed sound. Then she took a deep breath and blew it out. The breeze tickled her forehead and made her bangs shiver. She smiled gently, more subdued than before, yet determined. She tried the second key. It was one of her favorites, a silver oval that felt smooth in her hand. She struck it, echoed the sound, and tried the lock. Another failure.

And so it went, on and on for quite a while. Over a hundred keys she tried, yet none of them opened this oh-so-special box. Trick was never one to be discouraged, though. Either she had a key for this box or she would find it. This box, she vowed never to forget—though she would, given

A Shiny for Trick

enough time, if she left it today. Her memory was not the best. If she didn't keep speaking her own name, she'd forget that, too.

It was a rather unremarkable key that unlocked the remarkable box. An iron, knobby key that looked quite old. She'd been carrying that one for a while, though of course, it always seemed like a fresh one to her. When the key slid into the lock, she giggled and held it there. Sometimes a key fit the lock but didn't turn, so she tried without success not to let herself get too excited. She held the key there, giggling softly. But she *did* get too excited, laughing and drumming her heels on the pier. Somewhere in the middle of her laughter, she turned the iron key. There was an audible click inside the lock, and the lid popped open a tiny bit. Around the edge of it, Trick saw only blackness. She sucked in a deep breath and held it, preparing herself for the grand revelation. Now that that was settled, she left the iron key in the lock—it had found its home, and should stay there—and retrieved her line of keys. This one was a necklace, so she tied it back around her neck.

A Shiny for Trick

Today's special object was a hair brush. Of course, Trick didn't know its real name. In her mind it was kind of like a weapon. A holding thing. Something to be held. With strange, bristly protrusions that tickled her palms when she brushed against it. Her face lit up in a broad grin. It was, for that moment, the most wonderful piece of stuff in the universe.

She danced about the pier with it in hand, brandishing it like a sword, swiveling it through the air, shouting at it, and throwing it. For several minutes, it was quite exciting. When its entertainment value diminished, she stuck the handle in her mouth and bit down. *Not yummy.* She made a face, then plopped the brush upon her head. The bristles got caught in her snarled up hair. She tugged, distressed, worried that it might get stuck up there forever. She whimpered and pulled, though it hurt her scalp.

When at last the thing came free, she stared at it, orange eyes wide with surprise. She patted her hair where it had been caught and whistled with appreciation. Her hair had smoothed out. Several wisps of it were caught in the bristles. She touched them lightly with a fingertip and gazed in wonder. Somehow, this magical, wonderful item had made her hair different. It was smoother and felt silkier. She giggled with delight and put the bristles back to her head. She walked away from the empty golden box — already forgotten — brushing her hair as she went.

Trick walked into the crowd at festival, watching the somewhat real people do interesting things. Most days, they just walked around. Sometimes they held hands. Sometimes they walked together, sometimes alone. Sometimes they only sat there. But during this festival, they were more alive than ever. They ran to and fro. They skittered from one place to the next, making excited, distorted sounds like talking underwater. They danced and bought things and played with them like she played with things. She blinked large orange eyes at them as she moved about. She even forgot to move the brush through her hair.

It was a long time before she noticed that she wasn't playing with her new favorite stuff. She held it out in front of her and stared at it. Now it just seemed boring. Her hair felt nice. She had no more use for this thing. Time to give it away.

Somewhere in the world was someone who needed this thing. This particular thing, above all others. Whoever it was would be desperate to find it. They'd be so intent on finding this lost thing that they'd become lost themselves and temporarily step a toe into Trick's world. It was the only time that Trick got to see their faces and what they looked like. It was also the only time that her not-quite-real people had colors. Brilliant, wonderful colors that made them stand out like beacons in the washed out negative of their peers. Like they *wanted* her to find them.

Feeling purposeful again, Trick started looking. She walked from one end of the festival to the other, whistling, singing, and humming. She wiggled, leapt, and danced, weaving her way in between shadowy ghost people. Sometimes she misstepped and walked through them instead. The thin, chilly mist that made up their imprints tickled her nose and her eyelashes and made her laugh merrily. Even walking was a game, sometimes. Trick held the brush out before her like a flashlight to guide the humans where to go so they didn't walk through her. They didn't obey, so she pouted. Then, overcome with a need to, she waved the brush wildly at an oncoming shadow person and made whooshing sounds, trying desperately to dispel the mist. It was silly and fun and made her laugh uncontrollably. The human didn't deviate from his path, though, and walked right through her. "Trick!" she yelped indignantly.

A moment later, he was forgotten, for up ahead lay the beacon she'd been seeking, sitting against a brick wall. "Aahhhh," Trick breathed, pleased. A wonderful victory for the mighty Trick! She struck a pose to the sky, holding the brush as high as she could, pointed straight for the sun. Her eyes fell back upon her target. The human appeared to be female and old. She had sad eyes that fluoresced between purple, green, and blue. The rest of her shimmered and glittered in colors unimaginable. Trick always thought they were pretty. Most importantly, the old woman had a lot of tangled up hair, a fact that apparently made her sad. Trick looked from her brush to the colorful lady and back again a hundred times. There was always a pleasant feeling of rightness when she found the person who wanted her stuff. Trick loved it. She lived for it.

She crouched next to the old woman and studied her face for a long time. She didn't get to see them too often, but the shifting, lovely colors fascinated her. The woman held a tin can in her hand and shook it. The can was grey as cans always were. Inside the can was a handful of coins. They rasped and clanked and made hollow, tinny notes inside the can. Trick's eyes drifted closed as she listened. Her head swayed back and forth, and she rocked on her heels. The brush smacked on her knee in cadence along with the tune. For a short time, her stuff was interesting again.

But suddenly the woman stopped shaking her can. Trick's eyes snapped open, jarred from her composing session. "Trick," she pouted, sad it was coming to an end. Her orange eyes fell upon her brush. She smiled at it, sensing that it was time. She set the brush down beside the woman and took a deep breath. Then, with a bittersweet smile, she pushed her no-longer-favorite thing onto the mortal plane and giggled. She stood and flattened herself against the wall, eyes wide and staring down as her face pointed straight ahead. Her silly grin felt

A Shiny for Trick

perfect upon her face. She waited. Any moment now, the woman would notice her gift. This was the fun part.

Everything was the fun part.

When at last the woman's eyes fell upon the brush, she blinked in surprise. For several moments she was frozen just like that. Trick tried desperately to contain her laughter, but it snorted through her nose instead. The lady set her can down then and reached out with tentative fingers. Halfway there, she retracted them to her lips and looked around as if afraid someone might see.

When she decided no one would—except Trick, but she didn't know that—she snatched up the brush quickly and smiled. It was a private, happy smile, the kind that humans get when they are pleased but don't want anyone to know. They all looked like this, when they got their thing back. Perfectly pleasant. They didn't know what kind of fantastic quest their thing had gone off on. At one point it was lost. Then it was magically sealed into its most perfect box with its singularly interesting key. Trick searched the world over for those keys. She appreciated—thoroughly—every beautiful, unique box. She loved the stuff inside the little boxes intensely for a short time, and then she set them free. And at the end of the thing's long road, they came home.

Perhaps the things gained something extraordinary for having been lost. A little bit of magic, perhaps. Or at least some experience with the world. A good view, for sure. Maybe they went on Stuff Vacation, and came back only when they were ready for Trick to take them back. Either way, Trick loved them. She loved the keys, and the boxes, and the stuff, and the journey that keys, boxes, and stuff took her on. She loved the moments like these, when people got their stuff back and grew quite pleased.

Relaxed, the old lady with the crazy hair touched the bristles to her head. She tugged gently, holding her hair at the roots so as not to pull her scalp. Stroke after stroke, she unsnarled the knots in her hair. Trick watched openmouthed and in awe. Before long, the lady's wild hair was luminous and looked quite soft. Trick thought about touching it, but just then, the colors started to bleed away. The lady had her thing back, and she was headed back to firmly anchor in her own world, to become just another image that wasn't quite there. Trick watched her go with only a little bit of sadness. After all, she couldn't stay sad if that person was so very happy. She huffed out a short laugh and came away from the wall.

Time for the next box.

CHAPTER THREE
Of Sweet Music and Magic

The festival was ending, and the humans were up to something. They all gathered in one place and just stood there, unmoving. At first, Trick was rather upset by this. They were much more interesting when they moved around. Lacking color and personality, their movements were their only redeeming qualities while they lived in their washed out world. At least when they moved she could play with them—chase them, walk with them, run through them, dance around them. When they stood still, they were pretty boring. She watched, waiting for them to do something. Stubbornly, they refused. They yet remained in a large knot, standing and staring at nothing.

Yep. Pretty boring.

She was just getting ready to leave the festival and all of its supremely uninteresting folk when the music started. It began with a man's voice, soft and sad but kind of hopeful. Even garbled as the humans' speech often was, it sounded beautiful. Trick shut her eyes and listened intently, still and silent as a morning pond. A piano added its glory to the voice and together they made the sweetest music. Trick's head tipped side to side with the tempo. When the drums came in a few measures later, Trick turned back toward her now-less-boring humans. She understood now. They had gathered to hear the song, as she now turned to join them in it. She frolicked through the thick mass of silvery, flashing shapes to get to the front. She stopped about seven rows back. She was too short to see over the stage. Instead, she flopped down in the middle of the swaying throng, crossing her legs and crossing her hands over her lap. She gripped one knee in each palm and rocked side to side with rhythm of the song.

They had some kind of instrument that

sounded like her jangling keys. She wanted it *very* badly. Unfortunately, it was impossible for her to take things from the human world, so she was doomed to survive without unless one of her magical boxes was especially giving. She wished for it with all of her heart. "Trick," she murmured, enchanted, overwhelmed by the wonder of such sweet music. As the song continued, it gained drama and intensity. Trick jingled her rows of keys with the rhythm of the instrument she wanted.

Long before she was ready, the song ended. She pouted and whined, though no one heard her. She thought about leaving, but she'd thought that already and was glad she had stayed. Instead, she made up her mind to stay as long as this particular group of humans stayed, too. It ended up being for quite a long time. It was a rare occurrence for Trick to sit still, requiring the most excellent of reasons. Today was such a day. And, though she had forgotten, days just like it happened every year in much the same way.

She was happy that she stayed. The music continued, though none of their songs were quite as sweet as the first. All of the songs had catchy tunes, though. Trick danced and sang and jingled keys. She laughed and smiled and rolled around upon the dirt of the open space. No one in the real world would ever know. On a different plane of existence, hundreds of people were watching a tribute to a band known as The Beatles. Meanwhile, a half a world away, an invisible Nomchai rolled among them and giggled with delight.

Finally, it grew dark. The music faded for the final time and the phantom band left the stage. Trick was sad to see them go, but it was definitely time. She'd spent too long already away from her personal questing. Somewhere out there were hundreds of magical, special boxes with exciting things in them people needed. She pushed herself up off the dusty open space ground. Humming the tune from the first song, she patted away the dirt from her clothing. Her keys jingled, reminded her of the tambourine she wanted. That gave her an idea, which made her grin. She hummed their first song. When the tambourine came in, she patted her belly. The keys jingled as their tambourine had. When the drums came in, she stamped her feet. Trick became a one-Nomchai Beatles tribute band playing "Hey Jude."

She was in the middle of the na-na-na-na parts when a heavy, thundering boom split the air. She squeaked and jumped several feet in the air, startled. Her fear fled immediately when she saw what made the alarming sound. High in the sky were showers of sparks in yellow and red. A moment later, some of the sparks crackled and fizzled into nothing. Another boom, another fount of sparks. Trick was amazed. She'd never seen anything like it. It appeared to be magic, like the kind a wizard might use. Only she was pretty certain humans didn't know any magic. That was why they couldn't see or touch the boxes.

Around her, the humans made warbling sounds of pleasure. Trick was glad she wasn't the only one who saw them. Missing such a spectacle would be a true tragedy. Nonetheless, she wanted to be closer, to see them better. There were some trees that poked up high in the sky that obscured her vision. That just would not do.

Trick clapped and rubbed her hands together with renewed purpose. She grinned, happy to be moving again, even if

A Shiny for Trick

she wasn't back on her typical quest. Then, without further delay, she cocked one foot out dramatically before herself and began marching in the direction of the sparks, this time singing "Let it Be" but without the words. It seemed more appropriate for the pace of her marching, slow yet jaunty. She flailed her elbows as she walked, singing and jangling all the way. She waltzed through knots of not-quite-there humans. The pier was the perfect place to watch fireworks, and it was there she would go.

When she found the pier, the golden box was gone. The boxes disappeared as soon as they left her memory. Even if it was there, she wouldn't have remembered it anyway. The gulls, too, were gone. They were daytime birds. Trick seated herself at the edge of the pier. She hooked her arms through the railing and leaned forward, slouching over the bar. Her feet swung and drummed against the metal pier encasement. She kicked it with every boom from the fireworks high above, smiling all the while.

Trick was worn out. Too much excitement for one day. She'd sung and danced and twirled her heart out. The cool lake air was comforting. The water lapping against the pier sang to her like a lullaby, punctuated by the boom, crackle, and whine of the magic in the sky. It was actually quite noisy, but sometimes there was silence to be found in noise. Her head tipped forward. She set her chin on the rail and smiled happily. Today was a very good day.

When her eyes drifted open, the world was perfectly silent and still. There was no wind to churn up the glassy waters of the broad lake. There were no gulls. The people had all gone. There was a certain perfect restfulness about morning. Peaceful, just before the chaos of a day, like the world was just as sleepy as Trick herself. It hadn't been like this for a little while now, what with all the celebrating. Apparently, the music and the sky magic was the end of the weirdness.

Just like that, the festival was over, and Trick was back to life as normal.

She stretched, tipping back on her tailbone with her arms out wide. Her feet kicked out over the water, pointing her toes. She yawned to break the silence, eyes sliding closed again, her voice catching on the highest note. The tiniest breeze stirred up then, kissing her face as if to say good morning. She smiled and hummed with delight, and then she blinked back into wakefulness.

There before her, on a floating raft a stone's throw away, was a faintly shining magic box. Trick winked one eye shut and squinted, still sleepy. Then she blinked the other eye shut, thinking perhaps she might still be dreaming. When both eyes opened up, wider this time, she smiled. The box was still there. It seemed an unremarkable box. From where she was standing, it appeared to be nothing more than ordinary, unpolished wood. Still, a box was a box. Trick stood.

She climbed upon the railing, feet arcing around the immovable bar. Her fingers curled around the top rail and she leaned over for a closer look. She wobbled and almost fell in. She squeaked and scrambled backward. She'd never been in the water before. Nervous, she scrambled backward away from the rail. Then she crawled forward on her belly and peeked tentatively over the edge. The water was as unassuming as it always was, even quieter today than usual. It rocked back and forth gently, tapping the side of the pier. It was hypnotizing in a way, to watch it sway. Water looked and sounded gentle. Trick didn't *think* it was dangerous. She reached down to try to touch it, but her arms were too short. She sighed, hanging there with both arms dangling down. Her head tipped up to peek at the box.

It was still there. *Waiting*.

Trick pouted, unsure of what to do. This had never happened to her before. The box was out of her reach. She wasn't much of a problem solver. Life was pretty simple for a Nomchai. Find key. Find box. Find thing. Play with thing. Send thing home. This was rather beyond her comprehension.

Nonetheless, magical boxes were her specialty, and she would try. She ran back to the park on the shoreline. The humans' children played here sometimes. Trick liked them very much because most of them were small, like her. She often pretended to play with them. Unlike their larger counterparts, the children were full of energy and life. If they ran and laughed joyfully enough, sometimes the colors painted them, too. They left streamers of pink and gold as they cavorted through the playground. But Trick

A Shiny for Trick

wasn't there for the children. Though she didn't know the reason for their absence herself, the children were likely in bed asleep. It was too early for most humans to be awake.

Trick found what she was looking for beneath the large basswood tree. Sometimes during the windstorms, the trees shed branches. This one had lost a gnarly limb that was twice as long as Trick herself. She giggled, excited already, applauding her own genius. She dragged the limb across the park, over the sand, and down the long, narrow pier. It took quite a lot of effort. That box was as good as hers. She was absolutely certain of it.

It took a little clever maneuvering to weave the large branch through the railing, but she managed. Grasping the very end of the branch, she reached out as far as she could, meaning to hook the box and drag it toward her. To her eyes, the branch should have been plenty long enough. Unfortunately, she didn't even touch it. The raft that held the special—maybe not special—box dipped and swayed in the gentle swells. Trick was quite displeased. This box was taunting her, and that was not nice at all.

She dropped the branch into the lake, blaming it for her misfortune. Trick didn't handle negative emotions well. She felt them about as strongly as she felt her joyous emotions, which was, to say, quite powerfully. Now, due to the box's unkind taunting, she was just plain mad. She started to question if she needed that box at all. After all, it was quite a plain-looking box. *Not shiny,* she thought. *Not even a little shiny.* The sun was beating down on the not shiny box and it did nothing for its luster. Maybe there was nothing good in there after all. She had nearly convinced herself to leave when she remembered something important.

What if she had the key to that box? What if she didn't try to open the box, and the key that went to it went homeless forever? Would not that make for a sad key? Trick pouted again, dismayed. She didn't like to mistreat her keys. They were very special to her. If one of them wanted to get to that box, she would have to help. It was only right.

Trick peeked over the edge of the pier again, at the water. It was dark, blue and green and almost black. She couldn't see beneath the surface and didn't like to think about what might be under there.

She looked at the box again. The faint glow of magical promise was still there, just as before. Not shiny it might be, but for some reason Trick had a really good feeling about that box. Maybe it was because she couldn't reach it. Maybe it was because she was sure it was trying to trick her by being *so not shiny*. Whatever the reason, Trick decided then and there that she would open that box. She was utterly convinced she had its key. And even if she didn't, she couldn't take that chance.

She peered down at the water again, suffering the worst pangs of fear she'd ever felt. Water was unknown. It had always been there, but it was so *big*. Much bigger than Trick herself. What if it ate her up?

If she died in pursuit of an extraordinary magical box, though, so be it. She didn't dwell on it. Without another thought or doubt, Trick backed up, analyzed the rail, and dove between the top and bottom bars. She flew out over the black water and fell right in.

The first thing she experienced was panic. The water was cold and flowed over her head. It pressed on her from everywhere. Instinctively, she knew not to breathe. Instead, she flailed both feet and hands, terrified and knowing she was fighting for her life. Amazingly, though, her movements were enough to pop her head back above water. She breathed in a lungful of sweet, real air. It made her so happy that she giggled uncontrollably, quite proud of herself for her courage.

She stopped flailing. It was a mistake. The moment her limbs ceased moving, she sank back beneath the surface and the water swallowed her head. It really *was* trying to eat her! Trick thrashed again, and once more her head popped up above the surface. It gave her an idea. As long as she kept flailing, she would defeat the water, not be swallowed, and make it to the box. She could do it.

Up ahead was the raft with the box upon it. The ripples from her panic made the raft spin a little and bob up and down. Despite that, it was much closer now. Trick got excited. She laughed slowly, like a predator who knew she had her prey. But how to get there?

It took her some time treading water to

A Shiny for Trick

learn how to go forward, but she did. It wasn't graceful or fun to watch, but Trick learned the basics of swimming and shuffled her way toward the raft. Her heart pounded faster the closer she got to it, until her entire body trembled with the excitement of reaching it. Never in her life had she ever been so excited about a magic box. This was one special box.

When she was close enough to touch the ladder, she whooped with excitement. She pulled herself up the ladder, surprised at how much heavier she felt out of the water. "Hm," she hummed, hanging there from the rungs. It didn't matter now. She shook her head, spraying water droplets, and grinned toward the box.

Much to her surprise, there was a gull there. Not just any gull. An albatross. He was huge and ugly, bigger than Trick. He didn't look very friendly. Involuntarily, she cringed, sinking back down the ladder to peek at him over the edge of the raft. He hunched, tucking his neck in and narrowing his angry, tiny black bird eyes. Then, his wings slowly unfurled and half spread. Even only half his size, the bird scared Trick. "Nyaa!" she whined, making shooing motions. Its only response was a series of deeper-toned cries like the gulls sometimes made.

She didn't know what to do. She'd made it this far. Turning back wasn't an option. But the bird was larger than she was, and meaner besides. Confused, she hunkered down against the ladder and waited, trying to come up with a better plan. She didn't carry weapons, nor did she know how to fight. For a long time, Trick waited, thinking and dismayed. The albatross fluffed its wings and ruffled his feathers. Then he tucked one foot up against his belly and stood there on the other foot. Trick found that quite funny. She giggled, peeking up over the edge of the floating raft. The albatross, for his part, stared at her out of one beady eye, head cocked sideways as if listening. He didn't laugh with her.

His loss.

Finally, Trick's arms tired. She couldn't hang on the raft all day. It did make her wonder why the albatross didn't have something better to do with his time than pester her and guard the box. Unless... unless that meant the box really *was* special! And then, she only wanted it *more*. Either

A Shiny for Trick

way, he'd been there way too long already, and Trick needed to have that box. With a deep sigh, she climbed to the top of the ladder. The albatross noted her intrusion immediately. He spread his wings halfway again and began howling.

Trick had had enough of his attitude. She copied his example, spreading arms and ears as wide as possible and waving wildly, whooping and yelling and shouting. The albatross silenced for a moment, its long, narrow beak hanging open as if appalled. Trick didn't relent. She circled the bird like a sword fighter, trying to frighten it away.

The albatross screeched and nodded its head up and down, beak cutting a sharp V through the air. Then, abruptly, it hunched over and fluffed its wings again, preparing. Trick thought it might attack her, but in the next moment, the albatross kicked off the raft into the sky, leaving Trick alone on the raft with her special or not special box as the force from its take off spun them all in a slow, lazy circle.

CHAPTER FOUR
Of Scary Things and Winning

Trick was happy to see the albatross go. It seemed that this particular quest was her most adventurous yet. Already she'd braved the dark lake water and fought off a bird much larger than herself. She was feeling quite accomplished. She watched the bird shrink in the sky as it flew away, right up until the moment it crossed in front of the sun. The light burned Trick's too-large orange eyes. She squinted and wrinkled her nose, shading her eyes with one hand. The albatross was gone.

Which meant it was just her, alone with her prize. Squealing with delight, Trick plopped down on her bottom in front of the wooden box and studied it up close. It was,

A Shiny for Trick

as she suspected, a plain wooden box. It was much like driftwood, greyed out and dry, almost like bone. Despite that, it was smooth. Not polished, but sanded for sure. Burnt into the lid were the designs of a hundred different kinds of animals Trick had never seen before. A couple she almost recognized, for one looked kind of like a dog, and another seemed rather like a cat, except spotted. There were birds, bugs, and fish, though she didn't know what kind. The detail was beautiful and intricate.

Trick almost wished she could keep this box. Though at first glance it seemed quite ordinary, the box was anything but. In a way, this treasure chest was almost more exciting than the others she had ever seen. Someone—the artist, or wizard, or whomever made the boxes—had taken a lot of time to burn the pictures of animals onto the lid. She pressed reverent fingers to the blackened grooves, cooing to the box as if it could hear her. If she had the words to tell it how beautiful it was, Trick would. She savored the moment, as she did with every box. However, despite this being the single most special magic box she'd ever found, she remembered the albatross—though faintly—

and didn't want to be here in case he decided to come back.

Trick tipped forward at the waist and pressed her lips to the lid between her hands. Time to get to work.

She started with the keys at her wrists, flinging down the tattered purple ribbon. It fell in a sinuous yet haphazard line. Trick grinned with approval, eyes half lidded with pleasure. This was her favorite game. Frustrating, but so worth it every time. She waggled her fingers in the air and sighed, then started at the end. A round brass key. Nothing too fancy. There was an imprint of an evergreen on it and some words she couldn't read. She tapped it on the raft as she had done on the pier. The hard plastic wasn't as melodic as the pier, though. Instead of the metallic ring she expected, the key instead clunked and echoed. She was expecting the note, though, and was halfway through singing "Trick!" at the proper pitch. When the disappointing clunk happened instead, she snapped her lips back together and scowled.

She lifted the key to eye level and glared. She went cross-eyed. She hoped the key felt her disappointment. She took a deep breath

A Shiny for Trick

and firmed her lips together and blew out. Her lips made a funny sound. It upset her that the key didn't feel like singing today — because surely, it was the key's fault, not the surface she'd struck with it. Then she got an idea. She banged the key against the raft and made a *tock* sound by clicking her tongue. That pleased her. She giggled and grinned and shoved the key in the lock.

It went in but didn't turn.

She sighed with regret, the moment ruined. Nonetheless, she had hundreds of other keys, and one of them should work eventually. She worked her way through every key on the purple ribbon, sharing in their music and wishing one of them would find its home here with this loveliest of boxes.

As she ran out of keys, a gloom came over her. It was not unusual for Trick to find a box that didn't match one of her keys. Every one of the unopened boxes upset her. But this box in particular upset her the most. She'd worked hard for this one. She'd braved the lake and learned to swim, then fought off a monster albatross. This box belonged to her. She had to have it, no matter the cost.

A Shiny for Trick

She came upon her very last key. It was an oddly shaped key. The handle of it was shaped like a tipped over hourglass. There were several holes punched through it. The key shaft was a cylindrical bar, and the key's teeth were sharply cut and perfect. It had to be *the* key. It would be awfully cruel of the world to bring her this far and for all of her keys to fail.

But fail it did. Her final, beautiful key would not even fit into the lock. She cried in frustration and nearly threw the poor key. Her hand was flying forward when she stopped herself, frozen in midair like a still-frame. Tears bled from her eyes as she stared at her fist raised in anger, the poor little key caught in her palm. It wasn't the key's fault that it didn't fit the lock. Trick pulled the key to her chest and stared down at it. Such a lovely key. It hadn't been one of her favorites, but she decided then and there that it would be from now on. She could almost feel its relief when she decided not to throw it after all. Trick was sorry. She petted the key and smiled faintly. She was sad, but not angry enough to throw away one of her prized keys.

Finding momentary calm, Trick packed

A Shiny for Trick

up her keys. The tears were flowing, but she couldn't stop them. She stood, drawing a shaky, depressed breath of air. She stared down at the beautiful, unopened chest and died a little on the inside. It would tear her heart apart to see it go. She didn't want to forget.

Once she had the thought, it latched into her soul. She really, really didn't want to forget. If she left this box…if she walked away now, she would forget everything about it. How she'd fought for it, how she'd braved her fears. The animals upon the cover. She couldn't abide. She wasn't thinking about the consequences when she curled up around the wooden box. It just felt right. She would stay, right there, as long as she could.

Her patience ran out a few hours later. The raft was uncomfortable and cold, and she was thirsty besides. And tired. And so very, very bored. She whimpered, unsure of what to do. Though she hadn't forgotten how she'd braved the water to make it to the raft, she wasn't eager to jump back in either. When she tired of curling up next to the box, Trick stood. She paced around the box, glaring at it. "Trick," she grumbled, pointing to it, accusing it of being difficult. She was in the middle of giving it the what-for when the albatross returned.

Trick's response was immediate. She'd had enough of the albatross, and his attitude, and the box and *its* attitude. She stretched her arms out wide and glowered, hopping from tiptoe to tiptoe. She stuck her tongue out and made threatening noises.

The albatross's head swung from one side to the other, regarding Trick from its beady eyes one at a time. It took Trick a second to see that it was holding something. She didn't know what it was until the albatross dropped it to the raft with that same hollow clunk as before. It was a key. The albatross opened and snapped its beak shut a couple of times.

"Trick!" she screeched, amazed. She pointed from the key to the albatross and back again, eyes wide with surprise. The albatross fluffed its wings, opened its beak, and bobbed its head up and down, chortling and screaming at her and the world. Trick didn't know why it was so noisy, but since it looked like it wanted to be kind, she didn't complain. She reached out, fingers trembling, hoping it was being as nice as it

A Shiny for Trick

seemed. The albatross watched her but did nothing. It even tucked its foot back up against its belly and pretended to fall asleep. Her fingers touched the key. She made a fast grab and snatched it back toward herself, giggling like a fool. The albatross clucked once and went silent, leaving her to it.

Trick skidded to a halt in front of the wooden box and studied her new key. It was definitely the most beautiful key she had ever seen. It was gold—real gold, not just gold colored—but small. It fit entirely in her open palm, and Trick's hands were quite small. There were tiny engravings in the gold, but Trick couldn't read and didn't know what they said. If she could, she'd have seen *"Believe something magical can always happen"* etched into the key. Despite not knowing, however, she loved it more than anything. She worried she might mourn to see it go. It was such a lovely key that Trick didn't even doubt that it belonged to this box. *Of course* it belonged to this box.

The box was extraordinary, and the key even more so. Logic would therefore follow that whatever lay inside this box was to be the most wondrous piece of stuff she'd ever seen. She was so excited that the tears didn't even stop. She grinned but didn't make a sound, worried that even disrupting the silence would ruin the beauty of such a perfect moment. Besides, she wanted to hear the key. Just the key, as it made its connection with the lock.

She slid the key into the aperture. It fit. She lost her breath, so excited that even her lungs rebelled. She swallowed, prepared for disappointment. Or elation. Or a combination of both. This was, without a doubt, the most intense opening she'd ever done. She peeked over her shoulder quickly to see if the albatross was still there. It winked open one eye as if to say, "Get on with it, Nomchai." She smiled at it nervously. Then its eye closed again.

She turned her attention back to the box and slowly twisted the key. For a second, it seemed to catch on something. Trick's heart skipped a beat, afraid it was the wrong key after all. She frowned, pushing harder. Then the lock clicked, the most beautiful sound in the world, and the lid popped open just slightly. Trick beat both fists into the air and whooped triumphantly. Then she dissolved in a fit of giggles, rolling around on the raft

A Shiny for Trick

with her arms around her middle. She got a little too close to the albatross. He hopped a few steps away from her and quorked with dismay. She'd apologize, but she didn't know the words.

Finally, when the giggles died out, she rolled to her side and looked at the box. The lid was still slightly open, just as before, waiting for her to let the thing out that was inside. She wriggled on her belly up to the edge and tried to peek through the sliver of darkness. She didn't expect to see anything, but to her surprise, a faint blue glow pulsed within. "Ooh," she cooed. She slid her fingertips into the tiny space, then lifted the lid.

As with every box Trick opened, there was only one thing inside. This was the thing of all things, however. The stuff of all stuff. It was a blue elliptical stone, lit from within and shining in slow ripples. Every hue of blue in existence lived within the stone. The black-blue of the lake, the summer sky, the sapphire of gemstones, the pale blue of midnight snows, the purple blue of dusk. For a prolonged moment, Trick could only stare in amazement. It was the shiniest of all shinies.

A Shiny for Trick

This was the best day of her entire life.

Trick hunkered over the box, basking in the bright glow of light that emanated from the stone. It felt like magic and sunshine and happiness all rolled into one. The light tasted of life itself. Trick shut her eyes. The blue glow shone through her eyelids, not to be ignored. It begged to be looked upon, so Trick opened her eyes again.

"Trick," she whispered reverently, dipping her fingers beneath the stone. The velveteen cushion it lay upon was soft, but irrelevant. All that mattered was the stone. She hummed as she tucked it into her pocket. Then frowned, for it didn't quite feel safe enough there. She tried the other pocket, but it was the same story. She waved the stone all over, testing it against her face, tucked into her belt, in the palm of her hand. She even tried putting it in her mouth, but was afraid she'd swallow it. It seemed she had nowhere to stow it that was safe and secure.

In frustration, she stamped her foot against the raft. The resounding clunk of her boot against the hollow plastic was like an announcement from the heavens. Trick's eyes fell upon her boot, a step forward. Her

A Shiny for Trick

face split in a broad grin. She tightened her fingers around the stone and dropped back into a seated position. Then she smushed the stone between her lips. She needed both hands to unlace her left boot, and it took quite a while with all the keys tangled up in the laces. Still, Trick unlaced her boot with the kind of quiet determination one might use to prepare for battle.

When at last the boot came free, she celebrated. She spat the stone out into her palm and grinned, orange eyes alight with intrigue. She had, in her hand, the most beautiful, precious thing in the universe. Hers, all hers. She sighed to stare at it, relaxing from the tips of her hair to her toes. The stone brought her tranquility unlike any she'd ever experienced. What a lovely thing it was! It was so delightful, in fact, that she decided to give it a name. Only she had a name, so giving the stone a name was the most profound reward she could give it for being so wonderful.

She named her stone, "Teal."

Trick dropped Teal into her boot. The stone made her foot uncomfortable, but she weathered it. It was worth it, so long as Teal was kept safe. Besides, a small amount of discomfort would remind her that Teal was there, so she might never forget. Humming a tuneless melody that was almost "Let It Be" but wasn't quite, Trick relaced her boot. She carefully returned all of the keys back to where they belonged, flickering one last glance of gratitude toward the key that had granted her Teal.

Teal's presence strengthened Trick. She felt brave, powerful, and serene. The water didn't frighten her anymore. She could swim it, so long as she had Teal with her. "Teal," she murmured, asking her new friend to give her the strength she needed to make it back to shore. She peeked over the raft at the edge of the water and scanned its bobbing little waves all the way back to the shoreline. It wasn't too far. She could do it. She tapped her boot toe. Then, she jumped into the water. The motions of swimming came much easier now. Trick sucked in lungfuls of air and charged forward through the water, determined to reach the shore.

And in time, she did.

CHAPTER FIVE
Of Chimes and Obsession

Swirls of blue of every color. Sky, robin's egg, ocean. Azure, cerulean, indigo. Every shade imaginable and some that weren't, and all of them in the palm of Trick's hand. Trick couldn't stop smiling, amazed at such a wonderful find. She lay on her belly in the grass of the park. Teal rested on one hand while Trick petted it with the other. "Teal," she cooed, eyes shining with happiness.

Teal was her new best friend. She loved everything about the little stone. The colors were gorgeous and oscillated within the stone like tiny waves of the finest blue glitters. Pixie dust, contained within a stone in the palm of her hand like magic. A wave of sapphire, followed by a rolling fold of deeper blue violet, dispelled by a push of pale periwinkle, over and over again like a lamp of shimmering blue. Trick followed the path of each new wave with one fingertip, following the colors on their endless journey in an infinite circle.

The glow from the stone was cool upon her face. Light was usually a warming thing, as from a fire or a hot bulb, but this light was the opposite. Like bottled winter starlight. For a long time, Trick stayed with Teal, mesmerized by the slowly traveling arcs of color moving through the tiny stone.

After a while, her position became uncomfortable. She closed her fingers over Teal and slammed the back of her fist into the ground as she gathered the strength to stand. She hovered there for a moment, poised on her knees and the backs of her hands, ears straining for a reason she didn't know yet.

Then she heard it, like the far off distant echo of a chime. The most beautiful tone she'd ever heard. She rocked back on her knees and cradled Teal to her chest. "Teal?" she wondered, peering down at the stone. The layers of blue shivered and swirled. Trick raised the stone to her eyes.

A Shiny for Trick

Something came over her, a whim, and she held the stone tightly and shook hard once.

And there it was. A quiet yet omnipresent chime, divinely gorgeous. Trick hummed involuntarily, her heart pounding. Teal made the sweetest music she'd ever heard, all contained in a single note. The note seemed to neither have a beginning nor ending, merely was. It sang over the lake and through the park, from the past and into the future, around Trick and the rest of the world. It was the single most perfect melody captured in one tone, at once instantaneous and never-ending. It seemed to Trick to be playing inside her heart as much as outside her ears.

The loveliness of the music affected her in a way she couldn't place. She ached and rejoiced simultaneously, for reasons she could not define. The sweetness of it made her feel as if the world was one large garden of beautiful flowers. Every shadowy flash of human being was the most compassionate of all mankind. Every color was at its brightest hue, every tiny living thing worth its life. In the sweetness of the note, Trick felt small, even smaller than usual. It was as if Trick were the smallest being in the universe, but somehow that was okay. It meant that she had a long ways to go. She had good work to do to make herself worthy of the glory that surrounded her. The honeyed voice of Teal caused Trick to weep, her heart bleeding out beauty and wonder. She was part of this, part of the world, part of all the great big beautiful things that surrounded her, and she was more or less overwhelmed.

There was a deep, rich darkness to it, too, though. A barely there thread of discord, only heard in Teal's echo, separate from its note. It was as if the discord chased the melody away and left a hollow ache in its wake. Coupled with the mellifluous nature of its other half, it only increased the beautiful heartbreak, and it left Trick shaking and weeping upon her knees. This music, this single note, was the most powerful sort of melody she'd ever heard.

Teal was even more special than she had at first imagined.

When at last the note faded, Trick felt emptier than before. She looked down at Teal, considering sounding the note again. Ultimately she decided against it. Such a wonderful beauty should remain rare, else it might lose its wonder. She kissed the stone

A Shiny for Trick

and returned it to her boot with a gentle smile, wishing her new friend a good night.

And it *was* night, surprisingly. Trick had no idea where the rest of the day had gone. Perhaps time was passing more quickly than before? But no, that wouldn't make sense. There wasn't anything to be done about it, though.

Trick, being a creature of magic, didn't need real food the way normal creatures do. She was fueled by the joy she gave to others, was sustained by the positive energy exuded by the people she affected. It was another part of the reasoning that drove her to find and return lost things. An instinct. Except that today she hadn't done that.

Trick was hungry.

And it was too late to find magical boxes.

And anyway, why would she want to worry about ordinary magical boxes when she already possessed the most wonderful shiny thing that could ever exist? Every other object seemed so pale in comparison. It wouldn't be fair to Teal to force it to compete with other stuff for her affection. With that logic close to her heart, Trick curled up at the base of the basswood tree and went to sleep.

A Shiny for Trick

She awoke sometime in the middle of the night. Her insides were aching deeply in a way she had never known. Trick had never gone without her quest for stuff before. Unfortunately, Trick had no way of knowing that that was what was wrong with her now. She dragged Teal out of her boot and leaned back against the bark of the tree. She steepled her knees and rested her hands upon them, cradling Teal in both. For many hours, she stared at the blue stone, watching the shimmering waves ripple and evanesce. "Teal," she purred, tipping her head to one side, a dreamlike smile upon her face.

Without her needing to shake it, Teal sang. Rather, it chimed. The same lovely tone pierced the veil of night, taking the edge off Trick's ache. She sighed happily and shut her eyes, letting the sound seep into her mind and tickle her thoughts. The music oozed like warm honey into the empty spaces within her, filling her with its beauty and dispelling her hunger. A new note chimed some time after the first. It was deeper, richer, more complex in some way. This new note chased away the first one, and it played upon Trick's heartstrings like a master harpist. Her soul hugged that sound tightly, wanting to hold it forever and never let it go. "Teal," she whispered again, her voice catching on it. What was it about perfect, beautiful music that made one feel at once both alive and dying? Trick didn't know. She only knew that she wished it would never, ever end. And that, if it did, she'd likely do anything it took to hear it again, just once.

Finally, a third note sounded, calling back the first and also absorbing the second. It became a three note harmony, sweet and sustaining and tragic all in one. It sent Trick toward sleep, gently tugging away all of her worries and sadness and leaving nothing in its place but perfect contentment. Trick sighed wistfully, hugging Teal to her breast like a stuffed animal and curling within herself. Within a few moments, she was asleep, and Teal's music faded into her subconscious, where it stayed.

Days passed this way. Teal's music kept Trick alive, all the while she only watched the lovely blue glow and the shimmering waves. Nothing else mattered but that Teal was the most beautiful piece of stuff Trick had ever held. She couldn't even bear to look away from it for longer than a moment at a time, and to do so cost a phenomenal amount of effort. She found herself yearning more and more for the beautiful, dreadful music only the stone could produce. She also could not abide the memory of it fading. The moment she started to question what it had sounded like, Trick shook the stone and listened to it again. Over and over again.

Trick never questioned it. She was a creature of fleeting existence, frame by frame emotions. Right now, Teal was perfect and life was fine just the way it was. It never occurred to her that there might be consequences for sitting out her daily routine. What bad could possibly come from something so obviously wonderful? Trick could think of nothing, and so Trick didn't fret.

After a few days, Trick began traveling, holding Teal snugly in one hand and skipping along. The jaunty motions kept the song of the stone in constant melodious companionship. Trick sang along, her head tipping this way and that to the beat she imagined. Life was wonderful, music was everywhere, just exactly as it should be.

And then she saw him, and stopped dead

A Shiny for Trick

in her tracks. Her mouth froze open mid-whistle, though Teal's voice soared into the atmosphere, unaffected. Up ahead was a man, except that he wasn't quite a man. He had eyes the color of the stone and just as shimmery, accentuated by black paint at the corners. His hair was blacker than the darkest night and yet in places purer than the whitest snow, except that it wasn't hair. They were feathers, wispy, curling feathers in place of hair. He wore finer clothing than any of the humans that Trick had ever seen. His hands were enclosed in leather gloves and crossed over his chest. Though her memory wasn't the greatest, she knew on an intuitive level that she'd never seen anyone like him before. He didn't change colors like the humans did. Instead, he seemed to be fully immersed in her world.

Trick had never seen *anyone* in her world before.

"Teal?" she asked tremulously, holding her stone more closely to protect it. From him.

The man up ahead narrowed his eyes at her. He squared his stance. Then, to her surprise, he spoke. His voice was not the garbled, muffled sounds of the barely-there humans. No. This was a voice of tremendous power, and it terrified Trick to hear it. "Hand over the stone, little one," he commanded.

Trick's knees shook. She held Teal even more tightly, knuckles paling from the force. She willed the stone to lend her strength, then shook it once so that its voice could comfort her.

When the note chimed through the air between them, the man clutched at his chest as if it caused him pain. He groaned and clenched his teeth, and a low growl emitted. "Give—me—the—stone," he struggled.

Panicked, Trick shook the stone again and again, jumbled notes in many voices tumbling out one after the other, both discordant and harmonic in oscillation. The man ahead of her crumpled to his knees, gasping in apparent pain. Trick didn't have time to worry about him, though. The power in his voice and his sudden appearance in her world frightened her, and she didn't want anything to do with him. She screamed, turned, and ran away.

Behind her, the man reached toward her in supplication. *"Please,"* he begged, sounding tortured.

A Shiny for Trick

Another time, another kind of person, perhaps. But Trick's singular concern was for Teal, and that man wanted what was hers. *No.* "Teal," she whimpered.

She ran for a long time, down roads and around corners. She cut through gardens and alleys, colors blurring past her. She ran through dozens of flashbulb burnt out humans, heedless of the cold mist that stung her face or their obstruction of her path. Blindly, she ran, tears pouring down her face from the raw, unrefined fear that plagued her. Someone was here. *Actually* here. And he wanted Teal.

At long last, when her legs were tired and nearly gave out beneath her, Trick found another park on the far side of town. Over here, there were more trees. It was further from the big lake. It was actually farther than she had ever been before. She'd never seen this park, either. Dozens of children ran to and fro, playing together. Pink and gold tendrils sparked through the air as they passed.

Trick ignored them. She climbed the wooden ladder onto the play structure. She crawled on hands and knees, staying low. Her heart pounded, worried that at any

A Shiny for Trick

moment, the man with the feathers for hair would find her and take Teal. She vowed to remember how the music hurt him to use it against him if he appeared again. Panicked almost to the point that she couldn't breathe, Trick collapsed in the middle of a blue plastic tunnel. There, she sat with her knees to her chest, her forehead dumped against one hand. In the other, of course, was where she held Teal.

"Teal," she whispered. She wept.

A Shiny for Trick

CHAPTER SIX
Of Forlorn Princes and Selfish Things

It didn't take long for her to get over her terror. She hunkered down in the playground tunnel with Teal for several hours. After only a few minutes, the panicked cadence of her heart slowed and calmed. She still remembered the man, knew he was bad, but couldn't quite put her finger on why. She watched the blue shades turn over and over within the stone in the palm of her hand, mesmerized. She took a deep breath, then sighed. Already she felt better.

In no time at all, she completely forgot the man with the feathers and fine raiment. She stroked the polished, glowing surface of the stone, feeling refreshed and renewed. In

A Shiny for Trick

time, she felt well enough to leave her tunnel. She clambered out of the plastic tunnel, her knees squealing where they stuck briefly to the smooth surface. She giggled, amused by that. She tiptoed her way through the wooden fort, eyes distracted by the passing children and their sparks of gold and pink. She squeezed the stone tightly in one fist as she made her way, completely at ease.

At the end of this fort was a tunneled slide. She grinned with delight. The other park had slides, but not like this one. "Teal!" she exclaimed with excitement. She shot down the tunnel head first, hands straight out in front of her. The dark blue plastic—like one of Teal's shades, she realized—glowed dimly around her. The sounds of the outside were muffled while she was in the tunnel. Inside, all she heard were her own shrieks of laughter—and the bright, clear, joyful note of Teal in her hand.

In seconds, she was deposited in the sand at the bottom of the slide, laughing uproariously. She couldn't remember the last time she'd had so much fun. That taken care of, she skipped away from the park, ready to be off.

A Shiny for Trick

Up ahead, upon a picnic table, she saw a box. It was a rich, dark wood with shining brass hinges and bindings. It gave off the faint light of magic, a pale shadow that was nothing in comparison to Teal's lustrous finish. She took one step toward the box and stopped. She lifted the hand that held the stone and stared, confused for a moment. She blinked, then glanced between the box and the stone.

She tried to have a mental conversation with the stone, but in her head it went poorly. *Teal, I have to go to the box.*

Why?

I don't know Teal. It's what I do.

Why?

Because that is what I have always done.

Why?

The keys…I have to open the boxes.

Why?

There are things in the boxes that need me.

Why?

Because someone wants them very badly

Why?

Because…Because…Because…

She didn't know. She didn't know why she did what she did, only that she kept on doing it, day after day. Another key, another box, another thing, another human. Over and over again, without end. And did she ever keep anything for herself? No. Did anyone ever thank her for her service to the world? No.

Well. She wanted to keep Teal. And no one was going to stop her or take it away. Her mind tickled with a dulled awareness, as if someone had recently tried to do just that. Was someone after Teal? She wasn't sure, but maybe. The thought of it made her quite angry. She stamped her foot and glared at the box, as if it were somehow guilty of that very thing. She scowled, then stuck out her tongue.

The box only waited. For her to approach it. For her to open it. For her to return its key to the proper lock, remove the thing, and take it home.

She refused. She turned her back on the box and walked in the other direction.

The dull ache inside was back. It had been slowly growing for some time now, but she'd only just begun to notice it. Teal's music did nothing to assuage it anymore, though she didn't understand why. Teal always made her feel better before. She stopped walking abruptly and peered down at the shining blue stone. "Teal?" she asked it, demanding to know why it had stopped making her feel better already. Only a few moments ago, Teal was happiness itself.

She studied the stone, analyzing, looking for anything that was different about it that might explain the problem. Teal glowed just as brightly as before. The same coolness touched her face when she shut her eyes and basked in the illumination. The same limitless hues of blue ebbed and flowed within the small stone. Teal was, for all intents and purposes, exactly the same as before. She shook it. The same beautiful tones pinged through the air, whooshed through the chambers of her heart, trembled within her soul. She felt it just as keenly as before. Except now…it felt less special than it had.

Tears came to her eyes. *Why, Teal?* Was the stone abandoning her? The ache within her festered and grew. Her muscles agonized for need of nourishment. Her head hurt. Her emotions were ruled by negative feelings. Nothing felt right. Not her. Not this place. Not Teal. She couldn't figure out why that was, though, not for anything.

Of course, she wouldn't be able to.

Nomchai weren't meant for such large understandings. It was not her place in the existence of things to break from her routine. She was meant to do exactly what she had done before: find things and return them to where they belonged. In keeping Teal and ignoring the other magical boxes, she'd disobeyed the natural order of her kind. She didn't know that, but she was being punished for it severely now.

"Little one," a voice spoke up suddenly.

She snatched Teal back to herself and looked up. She came face to face with the man from before. She didn't remember him, of course, though he seemed familiar.

He smiled at her and tweaked her chin gently. He seemed like such a kind man. "Are you alright?" he cooed.

She took a deep breath to speak, but she didn't know any words. She whimpered instead, her face screwed up in an expression of helplessness. She shook her head.

"I can help you," he promised, his head turning slightly to one side. He peeked at her out of one eye. It was beautiful, like Teal. It was blue in many colors and shifting hues constantly, slowly, lazily, like the current of a wide, fat river. He turned his head slowly and regarded her out of the other eye. "You would like that, wouldn't you?"

She didn't know. She took a deep breath, looked down at Teal and back up at the man. She shrugged, uncertain, but closed her fingers over the stone.

"I think you need my help," he suggested, his face overcome with concern. He seemed genuine enough, like he really wanted to help. "It's very simple, little Nomchai," he drawled. "Give me the stone, and forget all about any of this."

Give up Teal?

She thought about it. This man was in her world, and he was whole and real, not like the technicolor humans who needed her help before. That must mean that the stone in her hand was *his* stone, and she was meant to give it back to him. That was what she was supposed to do, wasn't it? Return things to where they belonged? To the people who needed them most? She'd never stopped to consider why they needed them. To what purpose would this man use Teal? Why did he want the stone so badly? Was he a good man or a bad one?

A Shiny for Trick

She stood on tiptoes and looked him in one eye, then the other one. She narrowed her orange eyes and peered deeply into his, trying to scry for the goodness in him. Did he mean either her or Teal harm? She wasn't sure. But the stone was apparently his. So she should give it to him, right? Her hands drifted away from her, beginning the slow ascent to the other, considering. Yes, perhaps she should...

"Give me the stone," he commanded, his hand reaching out. His eyes grew wide, and hungry. This time, his voice was laden with the same forgotten power from before, dark and deep. It scared her just as it had before. She jerked Teal back toward herself. It chimed, loud and sharp and harsh on the ears.

The man crashed to his knees with a grimace, clutching his chest. She stared at him in wonder, stared at Teal while he panted. She was surprised all over again that she had somehow affected him. This time, though, she felt bad about it. She reached out and placed her free hand upon his feathered shoulder. He froze at her touch, peered up at her from beneath salt and pepper brows. His blue gaze softened into a neutral greyed out shade of cobalt. He blinked rapidly several times. He smiled, crookedly, sensing that she was only trying to help this time.

She smiled back, nervous but unafraid now.

He took several deep breaths, righting himself. Then he squatted back on his heels. He still towered over her, but he was much closer to her level now. He was much less frightening that way, too. "You're probably wondering," he murmured, "who I am?" It was phrased like a question.

She nodded.

"It's kind of hard to explain. Let's start with a name. I am known to my folk as Vahler. I'm what this world would consider a prince, of sorts. Meant to rule over my folk once I've traveled every world and lived among them. It takes quite a long time," he admitted with a wince. "But it's important, my father says." He smiled sheepishly. "Do you have a name?"

She grinned and nodded, then opened her mouth. "T—" She stopped. Then frowned. "Umm…" she trailed off, thinking hard. "T—T—Teal?"

"Your name is Teal?"

A Shiny for Trick

She shook her head in frustration, knowing it wasn't the right one. "Teal," she said again.

"So it *is* Teal?"

She whimpered and shook her head, tears in her eyes. How had she forgotten her name? She made sure to say it often enough. It was special to her, her name. She'd chosen it for herself. She knew that much. So where had it gone? She stared at the stone in her hand, wondering if somehow Teal was to blame for all of this misfortune. She turned watery orange eyes back to her new acquaintance and blinked.

He smiled. "It's okay if you don't have one," he assured her, dropping both hands upon her small shoulders. The keys she wore shivered and jingled. It seemed like such an inferior sound to Teal's music.

She scowled at that, too. Her eyes fell to the glowing blue stone in her hands again. Teal had become the center of her universe. It seemed as if she was well on her way to forgetting everything else. She racked her brain, trying to dredge up what it was that she could remember.

Vahler. Prince. Teal. That was it.

And just then, Vahler's eyes fell upon the

A Shiny for Trick

stone again, too. His eyes narrowed and grew hungry as before, the time she'd already forgotten. He wanted it too badly, and it made her nervous again. She shook free from his grasp and staggered backwards, bewildered. "Wait!" he yelped. "Please, don't go, Teal!"

He thought it was her name, so she shouldn't blame him. But to her ears, it sounded as if all he cared about was the stone. He didn't care for her. He was trying to trick her into giving him Teal.

Trick, she remembered suddenly. Yes, that was her name. *Trick*. "Trick!" she shouted at him, right before she turned and ran again.

"No, I'm not trying to—"

She shook the stone, remembering that, too. He screamed in agony.

Trick ran.

CHAPTER SEVEN
Of Other Worlds and Forgotten Things

The ache inside her was almost more than she could bear. She hadn't opened a box in two weeks, and the magic inside her was dimming. She didn't know the root of the problem or what was happening to her. All it did was serve to scare her further. She remembered several things that she rolled around in her mind, over and over again, to make sure she didn't forget.

The man is Vahler. He wants Teal. Teal's music hurts him.

Teal doesn't want to go back.

My name is Trick.

"Trick. Teal," she said aloud. Every few steps, she repeated it, like a mantra. In

A Shiny for Trick

between those steps, she shook the stone, protecting herself with its music. Step. Shake. Step. "Trick." Step. "Teal." Step. Shake. Over and again, the only routine she could afford to remember, certain that it meant her own life if she forgot.

Meanwhile, her life was fading, for she'd forgotten the routine she needed to remember most.

She nearly tripped over the next box. It was blue, cuboidal and plastic. The lock was plastic but painted silver. There was a large pink heart painted in nail polish upon the lid. Trick leapt back from it and glared at it, holding Teal high above her head. When it didn't rear up or try to attack, she tiptoed very carefully around it, holding Teal aloft. She even held her breath, in case it was sleeping. Together, they slid past the offensive box. She turned as she rounded it, then backed away slowly. Finally, when it was out of her reach, she spun on her heel and kept walking. "Trick. Teal." Shake.

She did trip over the next one, catching her foot on the immovable magic box and flying over it face first. She reached out with both hands to stop her fall. The sidewalk skinned both of her palms and left angry red streaks that slowly leaked bright blood.

Trick pushed herself to her knees and stared at her palms. Her lip wobbled, unused to feeling pain. Coupled with the rising agony that she felt within, Trick was a bit overwhelmed. She wept, dumping her face heavily against her palms and pouring her heart out in tears. The tears stung her wounds even further. She wept even harder. She cried until she couldn't recall why she was crying anymore, other than her hands hurting and the feeling of emptiness that threatened to swallow her whole. She took a deep breath, then turned to find out what tripped her.

The magic box was painted grey iron, the kind that could withstand a vehicle running over it. It was the kind of box that definitely held shiny things. It glowed peacefully, the kind of composed rest that magical boxes often had. It waited patiently for Trick to try her hundreds of keys to open it up and take its treasure. If a magic box had a mouth, it'd be smiling. It didn't, though. For a brief moment, the ache in her gut subsided almost completely. Trick nearly wept again in blissful relief.

"Oh, thank goodness," breathed Vahler.

A Shiny for Trick

"I've found you at last."

Her head whipped around fast, and the agony returned, spiced with the fear and panic of his arrival. *Vahler. Wants Teal.* "Teal!" she shrieked, remembering suddenly. Her eyes darted in a frenzy, her wounded hands forgotten, searching desperately for her stone. For it was *her* stone, not his. She patted the ground around herself, heart racing frantically. "Teal! Teal!" she shrilled, beside herself with grief.

"You see," he said quietly as he bent to pick something up. "I didn't get a chance to tell you why I needed this."

Trick's eyes locked onto Vahler and the object that was now lodged between his gloved fingers. She gasped. *"Teal!"*

"My soul is in this stone," he admitted softly, smiling faintly. "It's a requirement, to travel between worlds. Do you understand?" His pearlescent blue eyes came to rest upon her, laced with sympathy. "Do you know what I'm saying?"

She shook her head, still aghast that he'd duped her somehow. She opened her mouth to protest. Nothing came out but a squeak. She couldn't find the words. Didn't know the words. And in that moment, it was the

A Shiny for Trick

most frustrating feeling she'd ever felt.

"Shh, hush little one," he gentled. "It's alright. Let me start again. My name is Vahler. I've just begun my life quest. Every prince of my people who means to rule has to go on his life quest before he may wear the crown. It takes many years…probably longer than your lifetime. Time is a little odd when you're skipping worlds." He chuckled softly, holding the stone before him. It glowed just as brightly as before, attracting Trick's eye.

She quieted, listening to him speak. His voice had a soothing kind of quality to it, and she was at once calmed. And his story seemed rather interesting as well.

"But skipping between worlds would otherwise rip a soul to pieces. Imagine learning *that* the hard way," he said with a short laugh, his eyes unfocused. He seemed almost to be talking to himself.

Trick found that amusing, and she giggled. It surprised her to have done so. She clapped one hand over her mouth a moment later, her orange eyes going wide. The smile remained, however.

Vahler smiled back. "We learned to remove our own souls instead. Now we

A Shiny for Trick

keep them in these little stones. Convenient, no?" He held the blue stone up between his thumb and forefinger. It caught a ray of sunlight and broke it into seven colors, shards of brightness that made Trick coo in appreciation. "Yes," he whispered. "It's pretty, too. I find myself intrigued by the colors. My mother says that she's never seen a prettier soul." His whole face stretched with his smile, then. Genuine happiness.

The ache within her receded a little, to see him pleased.

"The music you hear in it is composed of the threads of my being. The notes are mostly pleasant." He flicked the stone with his finger, and a note even sweeter than any Trick had produced from it suffused the area.

Trick closed her eyes and hummed. Yes, it was quite a lovely sound. It even did something to assuage a little bit more of her own emptiness. When the note faded, and her eyes drifted back open, Vahler was smiling at her.

"Yes, it can be quite lovely. But as you know already, it can be quite dark at times." His smile faded. "When you shake and abuse my soul, it strikes me with darkness, despair in its purest form. I feel all of those things at once. Beautiful, brilliant, shining hope, brighter than this stone. And the darkest, ugliest depression. Anger. Joy. Wonder. Panic." He tucked the stone into a pocket over his heart. Then he shut the flap of the pocket and fussed with a button. When it caught, he smiled and sighed with relief. He pointed to the button. "I have a button now, see?" He began walking toward her, graceful and purposeful. "This realm was the first one I wanted to visit, you see," he continued in a low voice, patting his pocket. "And I got so excited, I dropped my Amarai."

He bent before her and smiled again. "Thank you, Teal, for finding my Amarai."

Trick blinked. No one had ever thanked her before. She was quite sure of that. But something about it wasn't quite right. "Trick," she corrected.

He glanced away and frowned. "I'm not trying to trick you," he murmured, troubled.

"No!" she exclaimed. He looked at her sharply. She pointed to him. "Vahler." She poked his shirt pocket. "Teal." Then she pointed to herself and nodded once. "Trick."

"Aha!" he cried, understanding dawning.

A Shiny for Trick

"Your *name* is Trick!" She nodded vigorously. "Lovely!" He reached forward and grasped her hands between his gloved ones. "You're very special, Trick. I'll never forget what you've done for me. Without my Amarai, I can't even leave this place, let alone return home. I'm sorry, too, if I scared you before. I was scared, too."

Her eyes popped open in disbelief.

"It's probably hard to imagine," he went on. "What it's like to lose one's own soul in a strange land." He kissed her hands. "Is there anything I can do to repay you? I fear I might never be able to match what you've done for me. I can't exactly offer you the equivalent of my very soul, but name your wish, and I'll grant it." His blue eyes shone with gratitude.

It dawned on Trick then that he meant to take Teal away from her forever. A pang of sadness darkened her heart. Her eyes settled on the closed pocket, wherein lay the treasure that she'd regarded as the finest of all the things. What could compare to the glory of Teal? She knew that Teal belonged to Vahler. She even understood that she could not, for any reason, have the stone back. It had returned to where it belonged.

A Shiny for Trick

It did not belong with her. Vahler was so pleased to have his—what did he call it? An Amarai?—back that she didn't have the heart to ask for it back. And, she knew from the look in his eyes that he would not be giving it back, no matter how much she asked. Vahler seemed to have a kind of mysterious power in sound. She shrugged, helpless, struggling not to cry.

It distressed the prince. "Hush, hush now," he urged. "There's no reason to fret. The stone has brought you nothing but pain. I can see it in your eyes. This is a very *good* thing, Trick."

Had it? She thought about that, but her memories had always had a short lifespan. She could remember nothing but the wonder of its light and music. Teal had meant the world to her. She shrugged again, refusing to meet his eyes.

"Nomchai, Nomchai," he mused aloud, as if recalling a memory. "Let's see…Nomchai search the world for lost things, found in their sphere of existence within randomized magical boxes. Whatever is inside amuses the Nomchai, and the moment the item loses its entertainment value, the Nomchai then returns it to its owner." He stopped reciting and looked upon her again. "You didn't want to give this back," he observed, tapping his pocket. "And you've had it longer than normal. You must be hungry."

The word held no meaning to her. She didn't know the meaning of hunger or how it might affect her. She stared at him, unsure. At last, she shrugged again.

He hugged her tightly. "I get it now. I'm so, so sorry, Trick," he whispered. "My Amarai must seem like precious treasure to you. You couldn't give it up, which meant you've been ignoring your instincts. It is good that I cannot replace that. But," he added, brightening. "I think I have an idea." He dug inside his jacket, rummaging around. "You like music, I think?"

She nodded. That, she was sure of, at least. She hopped from one foot to the other. Her keys shook with her. She bobbed her head with the rhythm and danced a couple of steps.

"Wonderful! In that case, how about this?" He held something out to her. It was a long, thin tube. It shimmered the same way the stone had, but to a lesser degree and in fewer colors. It shifted from black, to pearly grey, to sapphire blue and everything

A Shiny for Trick

in between. It appeared to be made of glass. It was extraordinarily pretty, but Trick didn't know what it could possibly have to do with music. "Oh, right. I should show you how it works." He rocked back on his heels and raised it to his lips. He arranged his fingertips along the rod, covering up what appeared to be small holes. Then he took a deep breath and blew gently.

A whimsical, lilting hollow sound drifted from the end. Trick's mouth fell open. It didn't quite have the same raw power that Teal had, but it didn't ache in the same way either. Vahler's fingers moved, shifting positions and which divots he covered. The tune changed. "Ahh," she breathed, moved by the beauty of it. He played a slow, beautiful tune that cascaded through many different notes. His eyes were closed, and his whole body swayed with every note.

Trick couldn't help but sway with it, too. She was carried away by the tune. Her life became the song, and the song became her soul. She and the music were one.

But then, abruptly, it stopped. Her eyes popped open, jarred. The first thing they fell upon was the flute, held out between them, snugged between Vahler's slender fingers.

A Shiny for Trick

"Here, you try," he beckoned. His smile was warm and inviting, blue eyes shining in stark contrast to the black wings at the corners of his eyes.

She reached out to take the flute, fingers trembling, suddenly nervous. She was worried she might break it. It appeared to be quite fragile. Her eyes darted between the flute and Vahler's encouraging stare. She blinked and stuck out her bottom lip.

"Don't be so worried, Trick. It's much less fragile than it looks."

Encouraged, her fingers closed over it. She raised it to her lips the same way he had. She didn't know which holes to cover, so she selected a few at random. She took a deep breath and blew straight into the mouthpiece. There was an airy sound, a breeze rushing through the hollow center. No music. She pulled it away and stared at it. She frowned.

"You need to blow across it," he explained.

She put it back against her lips and took an even deeper breath. She blew gently. The breeze was interrupted occasionally by something trying to be a musical note, but it still wasn't quite working. Then, she felt the

A Shiny for Trick

flute twist within her grasp. Her eyes shifted in her head to glance further down the length of the flute. Vahler twisted it in her grip ever so slightly. The mouthpiece rotated away from her. The air blew across the aperture.

And the music happened. However, the note was sharp and rather icky. She cringed and shut her eyes. Vahler tapped gently on one of her fingers, then carefully peeled it off its position to let it hang. Removing that one smoothed out the note. It sounded beautiful. Delighted, Trick laughed and pulled it away, then grinned up at her new friend.

"Keep practicing," he told her.

She nodded vigorously.

"It was lovely to meet you, Trick, but I must be going. I have hundreds of other worlds to visit before I can take my father's place. You'll be alright now, won't you?"

He was leaving already? Trick's good mood wilted entirely. She'd never had a friend before. The photo negative humans were washed out ghosts of friends. No one else existed in her world. Now that Vahler was in it, the thought of him leaving it was a lonely one. "Trick," she pouted.

"Please, don't be sad, Trick," Vahler

urged. "You'll forget me soon enough anyway." His expression was sad and lonely.

Trick didn't think he wanted that, either. She leaned forward and hugged him, willing him to stay. Vahler could stay, and together they could write songs for the flute and the keys. He hugged her back, squeezed her briefly and kissed her head.

And then he was walking away, a dark silhouette of feathers and kindness against a pale sky. Trick glanced down at the flute in her hands. When she looked back up to see him one last time, he was gone.

CHAPTER EIGHT

Of Albatrosses and Music Not Quite Heard

Trick loved her new flute. Though it was fair to look upon and marvelously pretty, the musical instrument didn't distract her from her existence quite so deeply as the stone had. She kept it to her lips as she walked, fighting to emit the beautiful sounds she knew it could make. She didn't name the flute. It was merely a part of her life as much as any of her keys.

Together, Trick and the flute were a team. The music accompanied Trick always on her quest for magical boxes. The melody energized her, and she found more than one box each day. With her flute, Trick could accomplish anything. She didn't fear

A Shiny for Trick

anything anymore—not the water, nor the albatross, nor any other obstacle that placed itself between her and the magical boxes strewn across her corner of the world. Unbeknownst to Trick, she'd become the most accomplished Nomchai in the universe.

Elsewhere, beyond the realm of her memory, a certain otherworldly prince with his shimmering stone looked on and smiled. He needed to be away from this world, but the tiny creature was so emotionally charged that he was worried she might not survive without his Amarai after all. For a while, he watched her, a joyful creature at work with a noble and invisible task. How beautiful it was to him that such a being existed. Trick's existence was meant to bring happiness to those that had lost something. Such a thing was rare and exquisite. He was glad to have met her.

Pleased to see she was getting on just fine, he left her to her music and her task.

Trick's eyes fell upon a large bird out upon the horizon, winging its way toward the setting sun. It was bigger than the others, which made it interesting and drew her attention. On a whim, she brought her flute to her lips and played a lilting happy tune, inspired by the wings and the colors in the evening sky. She never took her eyes off the subject of her impromptu song, drawn to the strange bird for reasons she didn't quite understand. It was impossible for her to remember it as the albatross that had brought her a certain fateful key to open a certain wooden box that had changed her life forever.

As the bird appeared to reach the sun, there was a brilliant flash of blue light that trembled across the sky. It flowed outward in slow, glowing waves of every shade of blue in existence, so bright that Trick had to squeeze her eyes shut for a moment. The light shone through her eyelids, cool rather than warm like winter starlight. "Teal," she murmured to herself, then stopped. Blinked. She didn't know the word. Didn't know what it meant or why she'd said it, only that she had. She found this revelation peculiar, but didn't waste more than a moment on it. Try as she might, she had no memory of such a word.

But where had it come from?

It should come as no surprise that Trick of course forgot all about Vahler and the stone

A Shiny for Trick

she'd named Teal. Trick was a simple creature with a momentary existence. The stone and the prince who needed it weren't necessary to her life or her task. Before the day she'd been gifted with her flute came to an end, she'd forgotten all about them both, and was better for it. Now she was just Trick, and she had a flute that was far superior to the instrument she'd wished for once up a time.

For a Nomchai, Trick was quite fortunate this way. Most of her kind lived as mundanely as she had before. Keys. Boxes. Lost things. None of them had experienced an adventure quite like the one that Trick had. None of them had found a thing so precious that he or she could not let it go. None of them had risked his or her own life for such a wonderful thing, nor met the wondrous magical wizard who needed it. Trick had acquired rare worldly experience that nearly claimed her own life, and yet… now she sang and danced joyously to "I Want to Hold Your Hand" and contemplated stars and the worlds beyond.

Everything about herself mattered little and less, for neither she nor anyone else had ever bothered her with a necessity to know

A Shiny for Trick

—not that she remembered, anyhow. Her existence was merely that: an existence. It was a quiet, aware one. A private existence.

And that suited her just fine.

About the Author

S. K. Balk lives in the frozen wastelands of Northern Michigan with her husband, roommate, and two dogs. She works in the blood banking industry as a coordinator and in the laboratory, and writes in her spare time.

Printed in March 2023
by Rotomail Italia S.p.A., Vignate (MI) - Italy